Bhavana —
It was nice
meeting you!
Keep reading and
writing!
Lisa
Hallas

This book belongs to ___Bhavana g o M___.

Dedicated to my wonderful family who came up with this idea, supported me through this journey and helped me create these brave new characters.

Heartfelt gratitude to Elaine Culverwell, licensed marriage and family therapist, with whom I consulted for the age-appropriate positive steps taken by each character in these stories.

A Fearless Fifteen Series Book

HIDE AND SEEK

Sam the Snail Does Not Like Little Spaces

Sam the Snail likes big spaces. Big spaces allow Sam to move around and see the world around him. He likes to see fast birds, puffy clouds and pretty flowers. These make him happy.

Little spaces make Sam feel like he cannot get out. He cannot easily move. Sam is afraid of little spaces. Sam feels alone in his fear.

His snail friends are used to little spaces since they live in a shell. Sam lives in a shell too. But he cannot get used to it. He feels like he does not fit in. He is afraid, but his friends and family are not.

How can Sam face his fears? He sees his
friends staying in their shells while
playing hide and seek. He wants to play
with them. But he must stay in his shell
to play hide and seek.

He takes a deep breath. He tries to stay
in his shell for one minute. His heart
beats faster. One minute feels like a long
time. Sam takes another deep breath.
He thinks of things that make him happy.

Soon, the one minute has ended. Sam feels fine. Nothing bad happened. He takes another deep breath and stays in his shell for two minutes.

The time seems to go by faster. Why? The
time seems to go faster because practice
makes it easier. His friends see him taking
these big steps. They get excited for him.
When he sees how excited they are, he
feels great!

Sam continues to practice staying in his shell. With the help of his friends and family, Sam can now stay in his shell for many minutes.

Even though it is a little space, he now knows he can do it. Sometimes he is still a little afraid. But he will not let that stop him from having fun.

A Fearless Fifteen Series Book

WORRY FRIEND

Fred the Fish Worries About Everything

Fred the Fish worries about everything.

He worries about his gills not working.

He worries about his family staying safe.

He worries about other fish not liking him.

Be Brave

It is hard to have all these big worries. But he cannot help it. His father tells him, "Just be brave like I am." His mother understands how worried he is and tries to help him.

Fred does not know what to do. He cannot just be brave. He cannot stop his worries. His friends worry sometimes. But they do not seem to worry as much as Fred does.

How can Fred face his big worries? He talks to his friend, Rohan, to see what he does when he worries. Rohan tells Fred that he has a Worry Friend.

"What is a Worry Friend?" asks Fred.

"It is a little stuffed animal that helps me when I am worried," says Rohan. "If I am worried, it reminds me that I am the boss of my worries and I can tell them to go away."

"Does it work?" asks Fred. "If I close my eyes and think about shouting at my worries to go away, they go away," Rohan says proudly.

Fred starts to use a stuffed animal as his Worry Friend. He takes his Worry Friend wherever he goes – to school, to the seaweed park, on play dates. Fred's Worry Friend helps him to be the boss of his worries.

One night, at bedtime, he closes his eyes
and tells his worries: "I AM THE BOSS
OF YOU! GO AWAY!" He did it again the
next night, and the next, and the next.

After many nights of telling his worries to go away, Fred was feeling a little better. Now he keeps many of his worries away for a long time. He also talks to his mom about his worries, which helps him.

Sometimes Fred still has worries, "What if I cannot spell that word?" or "What if the new fish does not like me?" But he is not worrying all day anymore.

He likes learning new things in school.
He likes singing and dancing. He has
more time for these things now that he is
not worrying so much.

A Fearless Fifteen Series Book

SUMMER CAMP

Rosey the Raccoon Is Nervous Meeting New Raccoons

Rosey the Raccoon will start summer camp soon. She is excited about learning new things in camp. She will get a colorful camp t-shirt and will learn to sing camp songs.

Everyone is happy for Rosey. Her older

sister went to the same camp last summer.

She tells Rosey how much fun it was.

Rosey should feel happy.

But Rosey is scared about meeting new raccoons. She knows she is scared because it is hard to breathe and it feels like butterflies are in her tummy.

How can Rosey face her fears? She
remembers that she was afraid when she
started school too. But that feeling went
away once she made friends.

Rosey also knows that she is not as afraid around new raccoons when she helps them. Before camp starts, Rosey helps another raccoon on the swing and the raccoon smiles back at her.

At the store, Rosey picks up an apple that a baby raccoon dropped. Each time she does something kind or smiles at someone, Rosey feels sunny and warm inside.

On the first day of camp, Rosey stands in line waiting for the camp leader, Sally. Sally greets everyone with a big smile on her face. When she speaks, her eyes sparkle. Rosey smiles back at Sally.

When Sally is done speaking, Rosey notices another young raccoon next to her. She has pink shorts like Rosey's shorts. She taps the young raccoon on the shoulder and points to the matching shorts.

The young raccoon laughs and says,
"Pink is my favorite color too." Rosey is
less nervous meeting new raccoons now.
She knows she will make new friends at
summer camp.

Made in the USA
Charleston, SC
13 April 2015